Thanks to Nicki

by
Ann Howard Creel

★ American Girl®

For Joe

Published by American Girl Publishing, Inc.
Copyright © 2007 by American Girl, LLC
Printed in China
08 09 10 11 12 13 LEO 13 12 11 10 9 8 7 6
Illustrations by Doron Ben-Ami

Questions or comments? Call 1-800-845-0005, visit our Web site at **americangirl.com**,
or write to Customer Service, American Girl, 8400 Fairway Place, Middleton, WI 53562-0497.

The characters and events portrayed in this book are fictitious. Any similarity to real persons,
living or dead, is coincidental and not intended by the author.

The following individuals and organizations have generously given permission to reprint photo-
graphs contained in "True Stories": p. 104—top photo, courtesy of Cathay Liu; bottom photo by
Karyl Carmignani, courtesy of Canine Companions for Independence (CCI); p. 105—photo by
Gene Peach; p. 106—top photo, Gene Peach; bottom photo, courtesy of Sandra Barker; p. 107—
photos courtesy of Sandra Barker; p. 108—top photo, Karyl Carmignani for CCI; middle photo,
Corbis; bottom photo, CCI; p. 109—photos used with permission of CCI, Freedom Service Dogs,
and Wisconsin Academy for Graduate Service Dogs (WAGS); p. 110—top photos, Sandra Barker;
bottom photo, CCI; p. 111—top photo, Gene Peach; bottom photo, Corbis.

The CCI Basic Commands List used with the permission of Canine Companions for Independence.

Library of Congress Cataloging-in-Publication Data

Creel, Ann Howard.
Thanks to Nicki / by Ann Howard Creel ;
[illustrations by Doron Ben-Ami].
p. cm.
Summary: After a busy summer training Sprocket, the service dog she has been raising, Nicki's school
year gets off to a rough start as she works on reconciling her two best friends, accepting that Sprocket
will soon leave for placement with someone who needs him, and awaiting the birth of the twins her
mother is expecting. Includes essay on service dogs.
ISBN 978-1-59369-290-2
1. Dogs—Fiction. 2. Service dog—Fiction. 3. Loss (Psychology)—Fiction.
4. Schools—Fiction. 5. Family life—Colorado—Fiction.
6. Ranch life—Colorado—Fiction. 7. Colorado—Fiction.
I. Ben-Ami, Doron, ill. II. Title.
PZ7.C8625Th 2007   [Fic]—dc22   2007060706

Contents

1

Explosion

Sprocket trotted into my room. He's the service dog I've been training, and by now I know how to read his face like letters on a page. It said to me, *I want to jump up on your bed. Right now!*

I said, "Sprocket, no."

He gave me that sad look of his, kind of like a *What have I done?* look, so I got down on the floor and gave him some good loving behind his ears. As I was rubbing him and looking into his eyes, I couldn't help remembering. Before I learned how to say "No," I got myself into a big mess.

First, I ended up training Sprocket, even though my mother was supposed to—but couldn't because she was put on bed rest. That's because she's going to have twins later this fall.

Then I ended up working on a decorating committee for our end-of-school gala last May with two of the new girls in my class. I did all this in addition to my chores on the ranch and helping my little brother with his math. At first it seemed awful.

I reached up on my bed for my journal and

thought back to last spring. I looked out my window over golden pastures and green mountains to the blue sky beyond, and then I picked up my pen and wrote:

Sometimes things turn out better than you expect them to.

I put down my pen and stroked Sprocket down his back, where his coat is the silkiest. He let his tongue hang out and broke into a big doggie grin. I told him what a good dog he was.

Sprocket is a mixed breed, which is a nice way of saying that he's a mutt, but he's a really *special* mutt that was taken out of an animal shelter by a service-dog organization. He's a mix of breeds and a mix of colors, too—brown and black and white, sort of like a Bernese mountain dog or an Australian shepherd.

The people from the service-dog organization saw potential in him and entrusted him to Mom to teach him his basic skills. No one knew that Mom was going to end up on bed rest and that most of the responsibility was going to land on *me*.

I got back up on the bed, and Sprocket begged with his eyes to join me. Again. Most of the time service dogs in training aren't allowed on beds or on any

Explosion

Sprocket begged with his eyes to join me on the bed.

furniture, but Mom told me once that . . . well, every once in a while it would be okay.

I said, "Jump!" I couldn't help it. The word just jumped right out of my mouth.

Sprocket bounded up on the bed next to me. And then his cute face was in my face, and I just sat there for a minute with him, nose to nose. We needed to do some work on advanced commands, but for now I let him have a bit of downtime. Sprocket curled up, settled down on my bedspread, and put his head across his front paws. He looked up at me with his soulful brown eyes and seemed to say *Thank you.*

I touched the top of his head and told him how smart he was. And he *is* smart—*really* smart. That's the good news. The bad news is that he's doing so well in training that I might have to give him up soon.

Mom came into the room. She was so pregnant that it looked like she had a basketball under her shirt. Even though she was really big now, it was still hard to believe there were two babies in there. Mom didn't have much time left to carry the twins, and I didn't have much time left with Sprocket.

Mom said, "Are you ready for school tomorrow?"

I nodded. Tomorrow was the first day of school. Normally I would be excited.

Explosion

"Fifth grade, Nicki." Mom smiled. She tousled my hair and said, "Why the long face? Aren't you looking forward to it?"

Actually, there were a bunch of things I was *not* looking forward to. Mom was peering at me in a funny way that told me she knew.

I said, "I hope the teachers don't ask us to write those essays about what we did over our summer vacation."

"Why not? You had an exciting summer."

I tried to smile.

"You could write about Sprocket," she said.

"But," I gulped, "then I'd have to think about what comes next . . . you know, giving him away." I started swinging my legs up and down off the side of the bed.

Mom sighed, sat down next to me, and put her arm around me. Sprocket shifted a bit to make room for her. "Don't think of it that way. Instead of saying 'We have to give him away,' try saying 'We're turning him over for what he was always intended to do, to help someone with special needs—someone who needs him more than we do.'"

I said, "I know" and bit my lip. I knew that Sprocket could end up helping a kid who, for example, had to use a wheelchair, or one who was hearing-impaired, or something like that. But still . . . it felt as though he was mine now. He *was* mine.

Mom hugged me again, tighter this time. "And you could write something about how you made a new friend, too."

I nodded. But that was my other big problem. I *had* made a new friend, but one that my *best* friend didn't know about yet. Kris was one of the new girls on my gala committee last school year, and she had turned out to be really nice. While my real best friend, Becca, was away for most of the summer at her grandparents' house, Kris and I had become close. All summer long I had gone over to her house—a beautiful, shiny new home built in the foothills—and she had come out to our ranch. Kris had never been on a ranch before, but she wasn't grossed out by it—not even by the pigs, which are our main business.

"Nicki?" Mom said, and I realized I had been spacing out. "What's the matter?"

I said, "Nothing."

But Mom knows me too well. She could tell that something was worrying me. I thought about telling her all of it, about how tomorrow I would ride to school on the bus with Becca, as usual, but then when

I got to class, Kris would be there, expecting to hang out, too. And Becca doesn't exactly like Kris.

I finally looked at Mom. "Well, it's nothing that I can't handle."

Mom patted my knee and then stretched out her back, which made the twins stick out even farther. "Okay, but if you do want to talk about it, I'm here."

"Okay," I said. "Thanks, Mom."

After Mom left, I worked with Sprocket on the "Leave it" command. I had been reading about it in the service-dog manual. Graduates of service-dog training have to be able to ignore tempting things that they might come in contact with, such as socks, fast-food wrappers, and paper bags that look ripe for exploring.

Sprocket was full of curiosity and really needed to learn this command, but it wasn't a fun one to teach. I had to put him in a "down-stay" position and then drop treats all around him. I even used his favorite snacks, doggie pigs-in-blankets, putting them just within his reach.

I told him, "Leave it."

He looked up at me sadly, longingly, as if asking, *Why? Haven't I been a good dog?*

Something welled up inside me, and I could hardly stand it. I wanted to release him and feed him one hundred doggie snacks. I had to look away for a few moments, but I kept telling Sprocket, "Leave it," just as I was supposed to.

Sprocket was starting to shake a little, which meant that his frustration level was rising, but he didn't bark or whine, and he stayed in position. Finally I released him and gave him one of the snacks.

He gobbled it down.

Then we started all over again. By the third time, I could tell that Sprocket was beginning to understand. I even teased him a little bit with the snack, but he did as he was told. Afterwards I loved him up and ended the training session for the night. He had done well, as usual.

A few minutes later, the phone rang, and it was Kris. "I'm really excited about the first day of school," she said.

"Yeah," I said, trying to sound sincere.

"I mean, last year I came here in the middle of the school year," she explained. "This is my first time in a long time starting at the beginning." She sighed into the phone. "We've moved around a lot."

It's funny that Kris and I have become such good friends. Her family and her life are nothing like mine. Her father is a businessman, and her mother is an attorney. My father is a pig rancher, and my mother is a stay-at-home mom, except for the occasional home decorating she used to do before she found out about the twins.

Kris has already lived in five states. I've lived my entire life on Twilight Ranch, and for me, a day trip to Denver, the nearest city, is a pretty big deal. We're different, but we've become real friends.

Kris was still talking about school tomorrow. "It's going to be the best school year ever. I mean, now I have a best friend, too."

I had to swallow, hard. I knew she meant me. But I already had a best friend, one that I'd had since kindergarten, and I didn't know if I could have two best friends. Becca has always been my closest—and best—friend. She lives on a chicken ranch nearby, and until now it's always been her and me.

All of a sudden something started aching in my chest, and I realized how much I'd missed Becca. She had gone to Oklahoma for most of the summer to help her grandparents on their farm and to earn some money.

Then I felt something *guilty* creep over me. I tried to shrug it off, but it grew until I almost threw up my arms and yelled, *Guilty as charged!* I had taken up with someone else while my best friend was away.

I realized I was up, pacing the floor.

"Nicki?" Kris was saying. "You there?"

"Sure," I said and tried to brighten my voice. "I'm here. I was just wondering what teacher we'll get. I hope we'll be in the same class."

"We have to be. We just *have* to be."

"Well, we'll find out tomorrow. They'll have the class assignments posted at the school when we get there."

When I got off the phone, I sat back down with Sprocket and stroked his belly and chest, where the fur is fuzzy and white. He was asleep now, making soft little snoring noises. His breathing made his chest rise and fall. Sitting with Sprocket like this always makes me think better, and all of a sudden I had an idea. Maybe I had figured out what to do about Becca and Kris.

I had an old best friend and a new best friend. All I had to do was get the two of them to like each other, and then we could become a trio. Who says you can have only one best friend? Two is always better than one, right?

No problem.

So why was I swinging my legs back and forth again?

Explosion

I picked up the pen and wrote in my journal:

Everything is building toward an explosion. Sprocket will be leaving soon. My two friends are going to have to get to know each other and like each other, and soon I'll have two little brothers or two little sisters.

By the holidays, nothing will be the same.

2

First Day

In the morning, I got up early and went outside to help Dad with chores on the ranch. I brushed down a couple of the horses we board, and then Dad let me off the hook. He knows how busy the first day of school always is.

"Have a great first day," he said, stepping out of the horse stall he was mucking out. He peered over at me. "I'll look after Sprocket while you're gone."

"Thanks, Dad."

He stood still then and just looked at me. I saw something like worry or sadness on his face. Somehow Dad knew exactly what I was going through, too. "That dog has sure taken to you, Nicki. I'll bet he misses you today."

I said in a whisper, "Yeah." But that was all I could manage.

All summer long Sprocket and I had been inseparable. Every day we went on long walks, and I did training sessions with a little help from Mom and Mrs. Tate, the lady from the service-dog organization. I took Sprocket to Kris's house and out in public to teach him how to behave around groups of people. Through it all, he had done really well, and much better than I or anyone else had anticipated. He was alert, attentive, and mindful. He always waited for my commands, and he never charged ahead.

I thought back to the day Sprocket first arrived last April. Here was this big wild puppy that hadn't been trained at all. He had done some terrible puppy-like things, such as destroying Mom's down vest and chasing animals whenever he went outside. We'd both worked hard, and now he was almost ready for advanced training with someone else—and then possible placement with a new owner.

I knew that when we turned him over for advanced training, I would miss Sprocket more than he would miss me today. But I couldn't say it.

Dad said, "I'll keep him company when I can. You did a great job this summer, Nicki."

All I could do was nod, even though I thought everyone was giving *me* too much credit and not enough was going to Sprocket. After all, Sprocket was the one who had learned how to behave and respond to commands, and who had made everyone love him.

Dad said, "I don't want your mother to be out of bed for very long today."

I nodded again.

"Go on," Dad said and gestured with his head toward the house. "Go spend some time with Sprocket before the bus comes."

I headed inside, where Sprocket sat by the back door, waiting for me. I remembered when he used to bark and squirm and scratch the door, knowing he would get to go outside soon. Now he sat and waited, just as he was supposed to, and I could tell how excited he was only by the light in his eyes. In the middle of the dark center of each eye, I could see a sparkle, like a star.

"Hey, boy," I said. "Ready for a walk?" I reached down and stroked the top of his head.

Sprocket's eyes closed for just a second and then opened again. Bingo. Star-eyes again!

"Dress," I said.

Sprocket stretched out his neck so that I could easily slip on his gentle leader. Then I opened the back door. Sprocket waited quietly for my signal before heading outside. Then, as we walked out into the early morning sunlight, he moseyed along at my side, just as he had been trained to do. He kept his head up and didn't sniff at scents or try to chase critters.

We walked past our ranch's pig parlor, a place that reeks of smells, and headed toward the mountains

First Day

west of the ranch. This time of year the mountains are green on the slopes and gray at the top. There are some snow cornices—ice and snow patches that never melt—in the crevices, and they glare out of the mountain like stripes of white paint. Above the green and gray and white hangs a sheet of blue sky in a perfect color combination. A late-August morning on our ranch is just about the most perfect thing.

I looked down at my dog. The warm sunlight on Sprocket's black and brown fur brought out the gold in his coat. I stopped to hug him. "Wish me luck today, Sprocket," I said and buried my face in his neck.

I heard Adam's voice coming from the house. "Come on, Nicki. Time to catch the bus!" he yelled. My little brother is, as of today, a third grader.

I quickly walked Sprocket back inside, got him settled in his crate for a rest, grabbed my things, and then headed out with Adam. We had to sprint for the bus stop at the end of our road.

Our bus stop really *is* the end of the road. We're the first to be picked up in the morning and the last to be dropped off in the afternoon.

I took my usual seat on the bus and waited for Becca, who would get on at the next stop.

When I saw Becca step into the bus, I couldn't

stop smiling. It had been almost two months since I'd seen her, but she looked the same—the same ponytail of red hair and the same funky black glasses that made her stand out, but in a good way.

"Hey," she said. This was our usual greeting.

"Hey you," I said back. "I can't believe you're here. You were gone for so long."

"Tell me about it," Becca said and rolled her eyes. She adjusted her ponytail. "I got home late last night. Whew. Not that it wasn't fun," she said. "My grandma and grandpa are the best, but it's good to be home."

"What did you do?" I felt bad that I hadn't written as often as I had promised. Only one letter at the beginning of summer, and then I had gotten carried away with all I'd had to do. But Becca had written only once, too.

She rolled her eyes again. "More chores. Just a different set of them." She turned to look at me. "Hey, how's Sprocket?"

I sighed. "He's doing great. Almost too great."

"What do you mean?"

I looked away.

Becca said, "Oh." She knew that I would eventually have to give up Sprocket for advanced training.

First Day

She waited for a minute and then said, "Well, at least you had something to do, and someone to hang out with all summer. I bet you didn't have time for much else."

I had been thinking only of Sprocket, but all of a sudden my mind started working on that other problem. Kris.

It hit me that this was the perfect moment. I had to tell Becca about Kris and me. "Well, actually . . ." I said.

Becca looked over. "Actually, what?"

I stopped to think about my words, and then I just started talking. "Well, you know that girl, Kris, from the gala committee I was on last year?"

"The rich one? The one with the short hair?"

"Yeah." I drew a deep breath. "Well, you know how she kind of stood by me when the other girls wanted to let Sprocket go wild over at Heather's house and mess up his training? I told you how she was the only one who did that?"

Becca was staring and listening, hard.

And then it was like water running fast off my tongue. I couldn't stop talking. "Well, anyway, she kind of dumped them as friends after they did that to me and Sprocket, and then she really didn't have a friend, and then you were gone for most of the summer. So I kind of started to sort of hang out with her, and she came out to the ranch, and I went over to her house a whole bunch of times."

Becca was silent, and then she turned to face forward and stare ahead. But at least now it was out, really out, and maybe I could breathe again.

Finally Becca said, "So . . . you're saying you *like* her now?"

I had to say it. "Yeah."

Becca waited for a second and then whispered, "You like her a lot, like a good friend?"

I breathed out. "Yeah."

Finally she turned to face me again, and wow, Becca's eyes were shining and full of something, like hurt or anger. Her voice was creaky. "Like a best friend?"

I said, "No, not like a *best* friend."

Becca faced forward again. It was so quiet all of a sudden that I heard her breathing, and then she turned to me and said, "I don't like her."

"But that's kind of unfair, isn't it? You don't even know her."

"Unfair?" Becca's voice started to get louder and even creakier. "Are you *still* going to be friends with her? I mean, now that I'm back?"

"Well . . ." I mumbled, not knowing what to say. This was *not* going well, so why did I say "well"?

And then it was back, that water-off-the-tongue thing again. "*Well,* . . . I don't think it would be very nice to just *dump* her, especially since we hung out all summer long, and she doesn't have any friends, and she has been kind of nice and all . . . and I don't see why we can't *all* be friends. You'll always be my *best* best friend, but I do kind of like her, too . . ."

Finally, the words had all run off my tongue and my throat dried. I kept waiting to find out what Becca was thinking, but she didn't say another word the rest of the way to school.

3

Twenty-one Days

We piled off the bus, and Becca took off without me. I made sure that Adam was headed in the right direction and then caught up with Becca at the class assignment sheets that were posted in the main hallway of the school. I looked for the lists of fifth-grade classes. Becca was already there and had found our names. She was pointing at them.

She turned to me. "We're in the same class. *Again.*"

"Really?" I said and checked it out. Sure enough, both of our names were on the same list.

Then I had to do it. I looked for Kris's name and saw that she was there, too.

So all three of us were going to be in the same class. I didn't know whether to be thrilled or terrified. One thing I did know for sure—this complicated things even more.

Becca flipped her ponytail over her shoulder. "I see that Kris is in our class, too." She looked back at the class lists. "Yippee."

When she finally turned my way again, I could see that although Becca was acting *mad,* she was hurt.

Before I could tell her that I was sorry that I had made a new friend while she was gone, and tell her *again* that I still considered her my best friend and always would, she walked away.

I would have taken off after Becca, but Kris came running up from the other direction, pink-faced with excitement. "We're in the same class! Can you believe it?" Kris has short dark hair and huge eyes, which today were enormous.

I almost smiled, because it was great to see someone happy for a change. "Well, there are only two fifth-grade classes in our school. Our chances were always fifty-fifty."

"Is something wrong?" she asked, and I saw that her smile had changed to a frown.

"Nothing," I said and shrugged. And then

I decided to just get it over with. Just tell *her,* too. "Well, not exactly *nothing.* I have to tell you something. You know Becca, my old best friend? Well, she's back, and she's kind of hurt that I spent so much time with you over the summer."

Kris took a step backward. Her eyes had that same hurt look in them, the one I had just seen in Becca's eyes.

What was I doing wrong? This was not going well at all.

"Are you sorry?" Kris asked. "I mean, are you sorry that we did so many fun things together?"

"No," I said. "Of course not. But I guess I'm going to have to spend some time getting caught up with Becca, that's all."

"Okay," Kris said. "I get it." But she didn't.

Oh boy. No one *got* it. Now *I* was getting peeved.

A moment later, Kris was pointing at the class list again. "Hey, cool," she said. "I've never had a man for a teacher before."

"What?!" I blurted out and looked where she was pointing. At the top of the class list, it said, "Mr. Thomas, Fifth Grade." MR. THOMAS!!!

I'd never had a man for a teacher before, either, and I wasn't sure I wanted one. Every year my current teacher always turns out to be my favorite teacher of all time. Mrs. Baxter from last year was really special.

But now . . . MR. THOMAS!!!

What had happened to the fifth-grade teachers from last year? I checked the class lists again and saw that the other fifth graders were getting Miss Chesterfield. Then I remembered. The other fifth-grade teacher last year was Mrs. Vaughn, who had been pregnant—almost as pregnant as my mother is now. Obviously she had decided not to come back.

I couldn't believe it. On top of everything else, we were going to have a man for a teacher. And fifth grade was the year we would be getting the growth and development talk, also known as "the puberty talk," from the school nurse. Mom had already told me about that. So what would the man, our teacher, do during that? It was too embarrassing to think about.

All day long, while I sat at my desk, I could feel stares on the back of my neck coming from Becca and Kris, both of whom sat behind me. In front of me was this MAN, who was doing all the things teachers usually do. He took attendance and talked about classroom rules and stuff like that. But it was just so odd. He had short, spiky blond hair that made him look more like a snowboarder than a teacher. He wore a nice shirt and a tie, like the other men teachers, and he didn't really DO anything out of the ordinary. But I just didn't like him. I don't know why.

At least he didn't ask us to write one of those essays about what we did over our summer vacation.

It had definitely been the worst first day of school ever, and when I got home after a silent bus ride with Becca, Mrs. Tate, the lady from the service-dog organization, was there. I recognized her van in the driveway as Adam and I walked up from the bus stop. Suddenly, my feet got stuck on the dirt road, as though they were glued in place.

I couldn't move. Adam kept walking, but I panicked. *She's already come for Sprocket. He's gone!*

But the van was still there. Sprocket couldn't be gone yet. After a few seconds of taking deliberately calm breaths, I made myself walk onward.

When I stepped through the door, I saw that Mrs. Tate was sitting with Mom in the living room. Adam disappeared into his bedroom, but I went in to join Mom and Mrs. Tate.

Mom looked up. "Oh, hi, Nicki. Come and sit

down with us. How was school?"

I nodded at Mom and said hello to Mrs. Tate as I perched myself on the chair across from the couch so that I could see both of them. Sprocket trotted into the room, and I said, "Here." He came and sat at my feet. "Good dog," I told him and tried to fight the burning sensation that was building inside my eyes.

Mom said, "Good news today, Nicki."

I waited for this GOOD news.

"Mrs. Tate thinks Sprocket is doing superbly," Mom continued. "She thinks he'll be ready to go to advanced training in about three weeks."

My heart sank. Three weeks! But at least he wasn't leaving *today*.

Mom said, in the perkiest tone she could muster, "Isn't that great?"

Even she couldn't make her voice sound totally perky, but I could hardly blame Mom for being some-what relieved. I looked at her belly, and it seemed as though she had gotten even bigger during the day. I knew that she loved Sprocket, but he was one more creature for her to worry about right now. And even though I had done most of Sprocket's training, I knew that Mom still felt responsible.

I managed a nod.

"You've done a great job, Nicki," said Mrs. Tate, "stepping in as you did when your mother had to go on bed rest. I'm very impressed." She gave me a smile that I couldn't return.

I couldn't help it. I asked, "Do you think Sprocket will pass his advanced training?" I knew that if he didn't pass, our family would have first choice to get him back as a pet.

The truth was, I was torn. Half of me didn't want Sprocket to pass because I wanted him back. Especially today, when I was in danger of losing both of my best friends and when I needed Sprocket more than ever. As much as one of those kids who had to get around in a wheelchair or couldn't hear well, I needed Sprocket, too.

But the other half of me understood that Sprocket might have a special gift, something that could help a special person. So how could I be so selfish?

Mrs. Tate answered, "I think he has a good shot, as good a chance as any of our other dogs. But we never know until we get into the more advanced skills and he has a chance to work with other handlers. It takes a while for us to figure that out."

Whew! That meant I had more time, too.

After Mrs. Tate left, I took Sprocket outside and

sat with him in a sunny patch of grass in the meadow beyond the house. I let him lounge and nap next to me while I worked on a sketch. My only subject for the last few months had been Sprocket. I'd started this one while watching him during the last snowstorm of the spring. It had been playtime, and he ran around and around chasing snowflakes. He thought he could catch them. A smile rode up on my face as I outlined the drawing. I heard Sprocket heave a big deep sigh before he fell asleep.

I touched the grass between Sprocket and me; still greenish-gold, but very dry. Summer was definitely coming to an end. That meant ski season would start again soon, which was great. But it also meant that Sprocket would leave us.

How was I ever going to be okay without him?

Over dinner that night, Mom and Dad started congratulating me again, and I couldn't eat.

Dad said, "Mom told me all the great things Mrs. Tate said about Sprocket. You should be so proud of yourself, Nicki."

Mom said, "I knew you would do a good job, but I didn't know what an *amazing* job you would do."

Neither of them had a clue about how bad I felt. But then Adam looked up at me, and his eyes were teary. At least *he* knew. I think I had always known it: he had fallen in love with Sprocket, too.

Something started swelling inside my chest, a growing, expanding thing. Maybe it was everything that I had been feeling all day and hadn't been able to say to anyone. Now it was ready to burst. I tried for a few minutes to hold it in; I really did. But all of a sudden, I couldn't hold back that swelling any longer. I felt as though a trick had been played on me, on us, because Adam and I had fallen in love with a dog that wasn't ours to keep.

I yelled, "How could you do this to Adam?!"

Adam sat straight up in his chair and dropped his fork. "What?" he said.

Mom looked at me in a funny way. "Do *what* to Adam?"

Mom, Dad, and Adam—they were all staring at me as if I'd lost my mind. I fumbled for words. "Y-You know."

Dad glanced at Mom and then he looked back at me. He said, "No, we don't. What's this about, Nicki?"

I couldn't believe it. I was going to have to spell it out.

"The *dog*?" I said, yelling even louder now. "You know, the dog that Adam and I both LOVE? How could you just act like it's nothing to give him away in three weeks?"

They just sat there.

"I mean, how could you? Didn't you know that this was going to happen?" I glared at Mom and then at Dad.

They were looking very sorry, but they didn't say anything. And so I just waited. There was even more swelling going on inside me, but this time I pushed it back down.

"We do understand," Mom said softly after a few long, agonizing moments. "I know how it can feel. Remember, I did this before."

Dad said, "It's going to be okay, Nicki."

But I didn't want to hear any more. No more congratulations and reminders of how great it was that Sprocket was going to help someone else. How I would be okay. I got up, tossed down my napkin, and stormed off to my room.

Sprocket followed. Of course he did. He was sweet, sincere, loving, and always there for me when I needed him.

In my room, after a few minutes of working to

slow down my breathing, I called Becca and poured it all out to her. She listened, exactly like a best friend is supposed to listen. Like the old Becca. And there's nothing like a best friend when you really need to talk.

After we hung up, I pulled out my journal and started the countdown:

Only twenty-one days left.

4

Off to School

A week passed, and then it was twelve days and counting. But it was a special day, because I was taking Sprocket to school for the morning. Dad was going to pick him up at noon.

Service dogs have to be able to enter all kinds of buildings and businesses with their owners, but we had to get special permission from both Mrs. Tate and the school principal for me to take Sprocket to school. The principal had to check with students and parents in case of dog allergies or something like that. But it had worked out in the end, and this was going to be an important training session for Sprocket. It was also going to be fun for me, or so I hoped.

After my morning chores, I got Sprocket ready. I put on his service-dog cape so that people would know he was a service dog in training, and then I clasped on his gentle leader.

"This is a big day, Sprocket," I said and stroked him. He looked up at me with eyes that held so much trust. I let him give the back of my hand a little lick, which was his version of a kiss. He was sitting still and waiting for my directions, but I could tell by the light in his eyes that he was excited. He knew something special was about to happen.

"You get to ride the bus with me and go to school this morning."

He made a short smacking sound of approval.

Mom appeared at the door. "You know, Nicki," she said, "you can always call me early if it's not going well."

"It'll go well," I said, kneeling down to give Sprocket some last-minute loving.

"You never know," Mom said and sighed. "He's never been out with quite so many people in public for so long. All those kids . . ."

All I knew was that I wanted to be with him as much as possible while I still could. "He'll be fine."

Mom waited for a minute, and I could feel her eyes on me. "Remember that *you* have to decide when and if you want the other kids to pet him. Your class-mates are probably going to want to play with him. Just use your own judgment, Nicki, and be sure not to let him get out of your control."

"I won't." I stood up. "Don't worry, Mom."

Off to School

Sprocket followed my commands as Adam and I waited for the bus. For a change we weren't late, so I practiced the "Side" command that teaches a service dog to stand and walk on its handler's right side. Most of the time, a service dog is trained to be on its handler's left. But occasionally a disabled person might need the dog to stand on his or her right, for example, next to a wheelchair in the shower or in crowded and tight-squeeze conditions.

I was going to need that skill at school. When I gave the command, Sprocket as usual did exactly as I said. He moved over to my right side and walked just as he was trained to do. After practicing for a few minutes, I let him rest while we waited for the bus.

Adam put down his backpack and stroked Sprocket as the sun lit up the mountains with orange-pink light. When he stood up, he looked away toward the peaks. His voice was low and kind of shaky. "I wish they'd just come and take him now and get it over with."

I could see how he might feel that way, but I didn't. I said, "Not me. I'm glad we have twelve more days."

Adam looked over and rolled his eyes. We almost never agree on anything. We're complete opposites, but, funny thing, we both love this dog.

When Becca got on the bus, she smiled at Sprocket. She hadn't talked to me—really talked—since the night of the first day of school. Since then, she had listened to me talk about Sprocket when I needed to, but I could tell that she was still sore about Kris. We had eaten lunch together, of course, and hung out on the playground during recess along with Kris, but it had been kind of strained, to say the least.

"I didn't know you were bringing him today," she said and gestured toward Sprocket.

I said, "You didn't ask."

But I didn't want to fight. I sighed and said, "It's important for him to learn how to be in large groups of people and still focus on his owner."

Becca perked up. "Can I help?"

I sighed again. "Well, there's not a lot someone else can do."

"Oh."

"But if I need any help, you'll be the first person I ask."

She smiled.

As soon as we got off the bus at school, I saw Kris standing there, waiting. Her parents always drop her off at school. When she saw us, she ran up but then caught herself and slowed down so that she wouldn't excite Sprocket. So far he was behaving great.

"Hi, Nicki," she said and then, "Hi, Sprocket." She looked at me but didn't even glance at Becca. "May I pet him?"

I said, "Sure."

Then, as she knelt down and gave Sprocket some attention, Kris finally addressed Becca. "You know," she said, glancing up at her, "you always have to ask before you pet a service dog in training."

Becca put her hand on her hip. "I know that, and I just did that. I've spent a lot of time around Sprocket, too."

Uh-oh.

"Really?" said Kris, and she looked at Becca skeptically. "I thought you were gone all summer."

"I still spent lots of time with him. You know, like before I left and now that I'm back. And Nicki just asked me to help her with him today."

Kris stood up. She looked as if she was going to cry or something.

Oh great. Now what was I supposed to say?

Finally I explained. "We talked about it on the bus. Just now. On the way here."

Kris shrugged. "Okay," she finally said. "I get it." And then to Sprocket, "You're a good dog, Sprocket."

Just then, some kids came up to see Sprocket. I asked them not to pet him unless they asked me first. A few of them looked a little sore about it, but they did as I asked, so I let them pet Sprocket for a few minutes. Then I walked into school with Becca and Kris, but no one was speaking.

So much for having a fun day.

On the playground at recess, everyone wanted to get into the act. Having Sprocket with me today was giving me instant popularity, even with Heather, the other girl on our gala-planning committee last May. Kris and Heather had been friends last year but weren't anymore.

Heather asked me if she could pet Sprocket. When I said, "Yes," she crouched down and gave him some loving. Then she swung her hair over her shoulder and said, "He has gotten bigger over the summer, but he's still just as cute."

I smiled. How could I blame ANYONE for loving this dog?

In class Mr. Thomas, who had agreed in advance to let Sprocket come to class, asked me to talk to the class about Sprocket and explain why he was at school today. With Sprocket sitting attentively at my side, I talked about service dogs. I described some of the ways they could help people and how they are trained. Everyone listened intently and even applauded when I finished. Then I went to my desk and Sprocket curled up under it while I got ready to do my schoolwork.

Mr. Thomas told us that he liked to teach using games, and he divided our class into teams. Then we competed against each other on geography facts. I couldn't decide if I liked the game or not, but I was glad that I had memorized the names of all the Great Lakes—I won two points for my team!

Throughout the morning, Sprocket did great. Mr. Thomas stopped by my desk and asked me some questions. He seemed impressed by what I was doing. "I had no idea kids your age could get involved with training service dogs," he said.

I told him, "Well, I wasn't supposed to be quite *this* involved. My mother was supposed to do most of the training, but she's going to have twins soon and has to be on bed rest."

"Wow," said Mr. Thomas. "You and your family have been very busy, haven't you?"

I knew he was trying to be nice, but I still hadn't quite warmed up to Mr. Thomas yet. For some reason I wanted to say, "Isn't that kind of obvious?"

Instead I said, "You bet."

After he walked away from my desk, I heard Heather tapping two pencils against the edge of her desk. It's an annoying habit she has that agitated Sprocket last spring, but this time he didn't react at *all*. He had conquered distraction by noises. I was so proud of him!

During the last hour of the morning, the school nurse came in, and that's when I remembered. I had been so busy thinking about Sprocket that I had forgotten that today was the day when we were to learn more about growth and development, also known as "puberty." That word—it even *sounds* weird.

Everyone sat quietly as the nurse talked to us and showed us all kinds of diagrams. The room was silent, like a cave. This was sort of embarrassing stuff, especially with the boys and girls being together!

The nurse told us how we would have to start washing our hair more often and wearing deodorant, and she explained about the apocrine glands, which produce a milky substance in our armpits that can give us body odor. In the middle of her talk, Sprocket suddenly let out a howl that felt as though it came all the way out of the ground beneath him. I nearly jumped out of my chair!

Then I burst out laughing. I couldn't help it. The rest of the class started laughing, too. The nurse just waited, trying to hide a grin, and let us get it out of our systems before she went on. But what had come over Sprocket? He wasn't supposed to howl like that, but at least it broke some of the tension of the puberty talk!

It had been a long morning, and I could tell that Sprocket was starting to get anxious. It's hard to describe, but I can sense what's going on inside my dog's head. He started squirming a little on the floor and then picking up his head and setting it down again. He was ready to do something else, like maybe howl again. Luckily, the puberty talk finally ended and Mr. Thomas dismissed the class. As I was packing up all of Sprocket's stuff, I heard a smacking sound.

I looked down. Sprocket was chewing on some-

Thanks to Nicki

*Sprocket let out a howl that felt as though it came all the way
out of the ground beneath him.*

thing, but I couldn't see what it was. I reached down and pried it out of his mouth. An eraser! Where had that come from? And now it was chewed up into a thousand little pink, slobbery pieces.

"Sprocket, no," I told him. "Leave it. No snacks for you."

I looked up and saw Mr. Thomas staring at us. He gave me a smile, as though he found it cute or something.

You have no idea, I thought.

And then, on the way out of the school building, Sprocket sniffed up on a wayward potato-chip bag. I said, "Leave it," but before I knew it, he had the bag in his mouth. I had to pry that away from him, too.

What had happened to all our training? I had worked so hard with him on the "Leave it" command and thought he had mastered it.

Outside, as we waited for Dad to come pick up Sprocket, I began to wonder if Sprocket really could handle things like this—like being away from home for a long time in a strange environment.

Then something else began to happen to me, something awful and wonderful at the same time. *Hope* sprang into my chest. Maybe Sprocket wasn't cut out to be a service dog after all. Maybe he wouldn't pass advanced training. Maybe he would fail, and then I would get him back.

I felt hopeful all the way home.

When I got home from school, I told Mom about him howling and about the eraser and the potato-chip bag. I said, "Maybe he's not going to make it after all."

But Mom sat down next to me and said, "This was his first long outing in such an intense atmosphere. All in all, it sounds as though he did well." She patted my knee and said, "Not to worry, Nicki. He's not perfect—no dog can be perfect—but he's pretty close. Close enough, I think."

My heart sank all over again.

Later that night, in my journal, I wrote:

I trained him too well.

5

Secrets and Surprises

By the end of the week, Becca, Kris, and I were spending lots of time as a threesome, even though none of us had actually talked about it. I just kept sticking to my plan, focusing on both Becca and Kris so that I wouldn't think about Sprocket's soon-to-come departure.

The problem was that whenever we were together, Becca and Kris argued about almost everything. Today, they were arguing about Halloween. It was only September, but somehow the subject came up at lunch.

Becca said, "We always trick-or-treat in town. There's this little neighborhood right off the main street. It's our favorite place to go. We go there every year. All the houses are decorated, and they give out great stuff."

Kris snickered and then took another bite of her sandwich. She said out of the side of her mouth, "My parents think trick-or-treating is not such a good idea."

Becca bristled immediately. "Why not?"

Kris swallowed. "Dangerous."

Becca adjusted her ponytail. "It's not dangerous here. We know all the people in town. No one is going to poison us or anything like that."

Kris shrugged. "Have you ever tried a party instead?"

Becca and I looked at each other and then shook our heads.

Kris continued, "You can get the same amount of candy, and you still wear costumes and stuff, but instead of being outside traipsing around in the cold, you have a big party at someone's house." She paused for a minute. "Hey, maybe *I'll* have a party. We can invite all the girls from our class. It'll be fun."

I didn't know what to say. I had to admit it—it did sound kind of fun.

But Becca said, "That's not what kids do around here. Everyone likes to trick-or-treat. That's what we always do."

"Are you saying that no one ever wants to try something new?"

Becca looked away and pursed her lips. Then she glared back. "I'm not saying that at all. We do new things all the time, huh, Nicki?"

I didn't answer. No matter what I'd say, one of them would be mad at me.

The rest of the lunch period stank.

That evening, Mom told me she had been in town for her doctor's appointment. She touched her bulging middle where the twins were. "Only about eight weeks left now."

Eight weeks. "Did the doctor tell you if they're boys or girls?"

"Well," Mom said. "I did have another ultrasound—that's done to check the position of the twins and so on, but . . ."

"But what?"

Mom smiled in a devilish way. "I think I'm going to keep it a secret."

Well, I hate secrets. "Come on. We don't even have any names picked out yet. At least if we know if they're boys or girls, we can narrow down the names."

Mom shook her head and smiled again. "Sorry. I want it to be a surprise when they're born."

I hate surprises, too.

Mom said, "Besides, sometimes the medical professionals are wrong with these predictions. I think we need to have two boys' names and two girls' names. Just in case."

"That's four names."

Mom sighed and smiled *again.* "I know that, Nicki."

On Sunday, I worked on the "Roll" command with Sprocket. That was one of the only ones he hadn't mastered yet. Mom had explained that a service dog has to learn how to roll onto his back for grooming, health checks, and belly rubs. I read up on the command in the training manual and then got started.

Sprocket looked eager. He liked to learn new things.

I started with the "Down" command. He, of course, obeyed and went down to the floor. Then I took one of those pig-in-a-blanket dog treats and lured his head over his back. This made him slowly roll over so that he could keep his favorite snack in sight. Once he was on his back, I said, "Good roll!" and gave him the treat along with a belly rub. He loved that and gave me a big grin.

When I was finished, I said, "Release," and Sprocket got back up.

I did it a few more times, and each time I tried to keep him in the roll position for just a second or so longer. He was doing great.

Mom came in to watch and then told me to do this three times a day and work up to a fifteen-second roll-stay.

We were getting close to the end.

While Sprocket rested, I helped Dad work on the pig parlor ventilator that had been acting up. I handed him tools and carried things back and forth from his work area inside the barn. I tried not to breathe too deeply. Even though the pig parlor is self-contained for the most part, I could still smell the pigs.

After we finished, Dad asked me to go for a ride. He tacked up one of the horses we stable and board while I saddled my horse, Jackson.

Jackson's tight scratchy skin is so different from Sprocket's soft fur, but I love touching him and watching the ripple that moves down his flank as I do it. It was a good thing that *he* wouldn't be going away a week from tomorrow.

Jackson is a great horse and a good friend, but Jackson can't jump up on my bed. He can never go to school with me or over to my friends' houses. He can't sleep in the house and be there when I wake up—all the things that only Sprocket can do.

Dad and I rode side by side. When we reached the edge of an open meadow, the sun was so bright, it stung my eyes.

Dad suggested, "Let's gallop, Nicki. It'll make you feel better. I want to see you laugh again."

We spurred the horses into a canter and then into a full gallop. The wind was warm and fresh on my face, but it held the first cool tinge of fall in it, too. Usually running Jackson made me happy; Dad was right about that. But today the sharp ache in my chest wouldn't soften, no matter what I did. When we reined the horses to a halt, tears streamed down my cheeks.

Dad waited for a few minutes, just watching me and squinting into the sunlight. Finally he said, "It's going to get better. I promise you, Nicki. Time *will* make it better."

I gulped and wiped my tears away as quickly as I could. "I'm okay, Dad. It was just the wind or some dust in my eyes. I'm really okay."

He looked at me and wouldn't stop. "You can talk to me or your mother anytime, you know."

I reached down and stroked Jackson. "I know."

We rode until we reached the first low humps

where the foothills begin. We stopped for lunch at the spot where I often take Sprocket. It was there that a yellow butterfly had caught Sprocket's attention last spring and had almost landed on his nose. Luckily I'd had my sketchbook with me that day, and now I had that moment captured on paper, hanging on the wall in my room.

Dad said, "So, what about some names for the twins? You're so creative. What do you think?"

I sighed. "To tell the truth, I have no idea. It would help if Mom would tell us if they're boys or girls."

He smiled sheepishly.

I said, "Do you know?"

"I don't. Really, I don't."

We sat and ate sandwiches while the sun poured down on us. Then I said, "I know—Coca and Cola."

Dad laughed. He was munching on some chips. He lifted a chip into the air and waved it around. He said, "Cheeto and Frito."

Then I said, "Kit and Kat."

Dad thought for a minute, then grinned. "Ham and Eggs?"

My turn. "Flip and Flop? Trick and Treat?"

Finally I was laughing.

Dad rode back to the ranch, but I stayed out on Jackson for most of the afternoon. I missed Sprocket, but I was going to have to learn how to have fun without him. I made myself stay out later and later.

It was almost dusk when I turned back. I could see the very first stars winking in the sky, but even that made me sad because they reminded me of the stars in Sprocket's eyes that wink when he's excited.

Becca called after dinner, and after we had talked for a few minutes, she said, "Wasn't that a lame idea Kris had about a Halloween party instead of trick-or-treating?"

My plan to get Kris and Becca to like each other sure wasn't working. I fell on my bed and stretched out on my back. I tried to make my voice sound normal. "I don't know. Maybe it's not such a bad thing to do something different."

"Not on Halloween. I mean, it's a *tradition*. Trick-or-treating goes way back."

Finally I said, "I guess."

"So you agree with me?"

I was tired, and I was getting even more tired of

this. "Kind of," I finally answered.

After Becca and I hung up, Kris called, and she wanted to gossip about Becca. She said, "You know, it gets boring when someone is so closed-minded."

I got up and paced my room. "I wouldn't *exactly* call Becca *exactly* closed-minded."

Kris didn't say anything for a moment. Then she finally mumbled, "Whatever," and we talked about something else until I cut the conversation short.

Adam came into my room after I got off the phone. "I need help with my math homework."

I was exhausted after riding all day and after those two annoying conversations. And annoyed that Adam didn't even *ask*. It sounded sort of like a command: *I need help with my math homework.*

I said, "So what else is new?"

Why was I so irritated?

He looked surprised, and that made me feel a little sorry. But then he scrunched up his eyes and fumed, "What's up with you, Miss Manners?"

I just stood there. "You didn't even ask, or say please."

"I never ask or say please."

"Well, that's true."

We stood there for a few minutes.

Finally Adam said, "So, are you going to help me or not?"

My stomach churned. "Could you please ask Mom? Puh-lease, Adam?"

He rolled his eyes. "Thanks a lot, Nicki."

Great.

But it didn't end there. Mom agreed to help Adam, but only if I washed the dinner dishes, which hadn't been done yet.

"I need to put my feet up for a while," she said. "So this is a good compromise, don't you think? I can help Adam from the easy chair." She smiled and left me in the kitchen.

In a flash I started to imagine what it was going to be like when Mom had two babies to take care of. Even more work would be dumped on me.

Dad walked into the kitchen for a glass of water and then headed for the computer in the living room, where he worked every night running our pig operation. I knew he had to keep track of records every day, but something really stormy was brewing inside me. Before he was done, I called to him, "Hey, Dad, why don't you do something *new* for a change?"

He turned around and looked at me with a baffled expression on his face.

Secrets and Surprises

I went on, "I mean, why don't *you* do the dishes tonight and then maybe help Adam with his math?"

"Nicki, do you need to talk?" asked Dad in his usual calm manner.

"No," I said. "I need to walk."

I hadn't even known I needed to walk until I said it. But I put Sprocket on his leash, took him outside under the shiny stars, and walked until my feet grew numb. The ground was already starting to get cold at night, and my hands were raw from holding on to Sprocket's leash the way I was holding it—like for dear life.

Only one more weekend left with him.

Just before bedtime I wrote in my journal:

*So it looks like I can't have two best friends, but I'm going to have two little brothers or sisters whether I like it or not, **and** I'm going to lose my one and only dog.*

6
Day Zero

A week later I woke up and felt the ache in my chest that had been there for so long now that it felt like an old friend.

Day zero. Game's over. Time's up.

Mrs. Tate would be coming for Sprocket today while I was at school. Mom had offered to let me miss school so that I could see him off, but I had said "No." I had figured out already that it might be just the tiniest bit easier if I wasn't there to watch him walk away with someone else.

Funny, the morning looked like any other day. September in the shadow of the mountains was Indian summer, with cool air in the morning and night and warm sunlight during the day. The aspen trees on the mountains had started to turn yellow-gold.

This was a season I used to love, because I knew that after autumn came, the snow could begin falling at any moment. Then I could ski again.

Day Zero

I took Sprocket for one last walk and was surprised to find that I no longer felt like crying. Every night in bed I had been crying into the crook of my elbow so that no one could hear, and finally all that was left of me was this empty shell of a kid on autopilot walking a dog. Nothing else could touch me now.

Back at the house, I gathered up all of Sprocket's things. I put his toys, his cape, and what was left of his favorite doggie treats in a bag and then shoved them inside his crate.

Dad came in before heading outside. He hadn't asked me to do any chores that morning, and I hadn't volunteered. "How are you?" he asked.

I was too numb to answer.

He said, "I know. Dumb question."

I whispered, "I'm okay."

"Well," he said, "it's okay if you're not okay. But it won't last long. Trust me. Every day it will get a little easier."

Adam walked through the room on his way to the kitchen. He made a snorting sound. "Yeah, right."

Dad followed Adam with his eyes, and so did I. Then Dad looked back at me. "Look, I'm really sorry this has been so hard on you and Adam. I don't think your mother had any idea . . . and of course, she thought that *she* would be the main trainer of the dog."

"It wouldn't have made much difference," I said.
"I mean, look at Adam. He didn't do much of the
training, and he still feels the same way I do. A dog
comes to live with you, and then it's like he or she
becomes a part of your *family*. A *real* member of the
family, only one that never talks back to you or ever
means to hurt you. Ever." I was losing it, and I couldn't
afford the time to cry. I glanced at the clock. Adam and
I needed to leave for the bus stop in just a few minutes.

Dad was just standing there, watching me. "Well,
I'll let you say good-bye to Sprocket alone." And then he
walked away.

But . . . no good-byes. I couldn't do it. Besides,
maybe Sprocket would come back to me. This might
not be good-bye.

Instead, all I did was rub him behind his ears and
stroke down his back, just as I did every day before
I left for school. He looked at me just as he always did,
and maybe that was the worst part. He trusted me, and
he had no idea that from this day onward, his life
would change. He had no idea we would not be seeing
each other again.

I stared into his eyes for a moment. It had always
amazed me—his direct and open gaze, just like that

of a person who is trying to tell you he or she loves you. Then Adam was standing there, waiting for me. I tore myself away, grabbed my things for school, and said to Adam, "I'm fine."

He said, "Yeah, right," again.

At school, I hadn't been sitting at my desk for more than a few minutes before I noticed that Mr. Thomas was looking at me in an odd way. During silent reading time, he came by my desk. He crouched down. "Anything wrong, Nicki?"

"No," I said. "I'm fine."

"I noticed that you aren't reading," he said in a quiet, soft voice. "You haven't turned a single page. And you're really fidgety today."

Wow, I had to snap out of this. Everyone was noticing. I saw the boy who sits next to me watching and trying to listen in on our conversation. "Sorry," I finally said to Mr. Thomas and tried to sound strong and determined. "I'll read. No problem."

"You're not in trouble, Nicki," Mr. Thomas replied, softly again, and then he waited for a second. "I just wondered if anything was wrong, if there was anything that I could do . . ."

"No," I said and tried to look and sound cheery then. "Nothing. I was just thinking, that's all. You know, some girl stuff. You wouldn't understand. But I'm fine. Really fine."

He stood up slowly after another second or so. "Okay," he said.

"Thanks for asking, though."

He smiled. "You're welcome."

I turned back to my book, the one I was supposed to be reading, but the page was blurry.

At recess, Kris and Becca were actually being a little bit nice to each other. Of course both of them knew that Sprocket was leaving today, that he would be gone when I got home, and maybe, just maybe, they were being nice to each other for my benefit. Just to help me out a little bit.

When recess was almost over, Kris said, "Hey, I have a good idea. Do you want to come over to my house after school?" She was looking at me and Becca.

Cool.

I thought that was a great idea. Adam could tell Mom I had gone home with Kris, and that way I could avoid going back to the house that no longer held Sprocket. I could avoid it for a little while longer, and

I might even have some *fun,* or think about something else for a change.

I said, "I want to come. Thanks!" Then I looked at Becca.

She glanced away for just a moment, but then she said, "I'll come, too. Good idea, Kris."

At least something was going right.

But once we got over to Kris's house, I could see that Becca was upset. I realized that she had probably never been inside one of the perfect new homes that hug the hills outside our town. I had sort of gotten used to it over the summer hanging out with Kris.

But Becca was just now seeing how shiny and just plain RICH these houses are on the inside, too. Kris's house had a huge kitchen with marble countertops and pretty, pale wood floors. All the furniture matched and looked as though it had just been delivered from a store.

Becca shot me a look that said, *UNBELIEVABLE.*

We sat on the floor in Kris's room and started playing with Kris's cat, a yellow tabby named Pumpkin. The cat purred and rubbed along our hands and closed her eyes as if she was in a state of bliss.

Kris said, "Maybe you should get another pet, Nicki." She sounded soft in the way she talked, just as Mr. Thomas had. She stroked Pumpkin. "I mean, I know it wouldn't replace Sprocket, but at least you would have another animal to take care of."

I tried to think about it. Maybe it wasn't such a bad idea, but I didn't know . . .

Becca was trying to be nice, too. She said, "Yeah, we could go to the animal shelter, and maybe there would be another dog that even looks a little like Sprocket."

I tried to think about that.

Kris straightened her back and said, "I didn't mean another *dog.* I think that's the worst thing Nicki could do. I was thinking of something completely different, like a cat or a hamster, or even a bird."

"Birds aren't cuddly," Becca said back. "And that's the part she's going to miss. All the attention and cuddling."

Their voices had changed, that fast. This didn't have anything to do with helping ME anymore.

"She's going to miss the company of a pet," said Kris. "Another dog would make her miss Sprocket even more. But a different pet wouldn't make her feel so sad."

How could either one of them know what I was going to miss or what would help me feel better, when even *I* didn't know?

Becca was fuming by then. "Another dog is the only thing that would help."

"I disagree. A guinea pig would be fun."

"That's a rodent. We're ranch people. We don't exactly *get* the whole pet rodent thing."

Kris was peeved now, too. "Guinea pigs are so cute. Don't you think so, Nicki?"

I didn't know what to say.

Kris was waiting for an answer that just wouldn't come out of my mouth. Finally she asked me again, "Don't you think something like a guinea pig would help?"

At last I found my voice. "Nothing is going to help." I looked from Kris to Becca, then back again to Kris. "Thanks a lot, you guys," I said.

At home I tried to go back in time and pretend that it was just an ordinary day before Sprocket had come to live with us. *Just think back to those days,* I told myself.

But it wasn't working. There was a big gap in the air, a big hole in every room I walked into, and it surrounded everything I tried to do. Maybe the hole was in my heart.

Before dinner I asked Mom if we could call Mrs. Tate and ask how Sprocket was doing.

She said, "I think it's a little too soon for that. Wait for a few days, okay? And then we'll call."

She gave me a hug, and the huge lump of twins bulged in between us, making it hard to get a good grip on her, even though I wanted to, needed to. Mom said, "Give it a few days first. Then we'll call, I promise."

"Why? Why do we have to wait?" I asked into her chest. "I just want to make sure they got back to Mrs. Tate's place safe and sound."

Mom looked sad. "Mrs. Tate would've called if there were any problems. We'll be in touch, never fear. Just not tonight. It's against my better judgment."

I nearly lost it. I was beginning to think that no one around me possessed any better judgment at all.

In my journal that night I wrote:

I can't help it. I hope Sprocket doesn't pass his advanced training. I want him back.

7

Time

For the first few days after Sprocket left, time stood still. Every day lasted forever.

But somehow I kept on getting up in the morning, doing my chores, going to school, and hanging out with Becca or Kris or both of them together when they could get along. At home I spent more time outside caring for and riding Jackson so that I wouldn't be sitting around waiting for Sprocket to come romping into my room.

Mom finally called Mrs. Tate while I was at school and reported to me that Sprocket was doing fine. No details, just that he was okay and adjusting well. I didn't know if I was happy for him or torn up all over again for me.

I had to leave the house and go outside to Jackson. On my way out, I grabbed an apple out of the fruit bowl on the kitchen table and shoved it into my pocket. Mom doesn't like me to feed apples to Jackson unless they've gotten old—they're too expensive for horse treats, she says. But today I didn't care, and Mom didn't say a word.

Thanks to Nicki

I found Jackson in his stall, and he stuck his head out to greet me. I ran my palm down his slick, hard forehead to his muzzle. He made a contented snorting sound, and his breath was warm on my hand. I pulled out the apple, which he sniffed once and then took whole into his mouth.

As he crunched it down, his eyes said, *Thanks, Nicki.*

I grabbed the curry brush to groom him, but then stopped and leaned my forehead against his. I just stood there with him for a long, long time.

Before I knew it, a whole week without Sprocket had passed, and then another.

Then it was October.

The aspen leaves fell on the high slopes, but at the lower elevations they still clung to the trees, now deep yellow. Every night was colder than the night before, and every morning frost crunched under our feet as Adam and I ran for the bus.

Time really was beginning to pass.

Mom had said, "Time heals all wounds."

I still didn't know if I believed that or not, if time healed all wounds or *any* wounds, but I did know that it just kept on moving by. In a way I was getting back to normal, even though I still hadn't figured out what normal was, without my dog.

One day in the middle of October, Kris, Becca, and I were sitting at the big lunch table in the school cafeteria. No one was saying much. We had just finished a hard spelling test, and after lunch we were supposed to have silent reading time. I felt a yawn start to bulge out of me.

Kris said, "So what *are* we going to do for Halloween?"

I stopped chewing my peanut butter and jelly

sandwich. This was out of the blue and it was also a bad subject.

I shrugged. I didn't want to get into it at the moment.

Becca said, "I still want to trick-or-treat."

Kris was munching on carrot sticks. Between bites she said, "I've been thinking about a compromise."

I sat up straight. This sounded promising.

Even Becca paid close attention. She asked Kris, "What kind of compromise?" Becca still looked skeptical, but I could tell that she was at least going to listen.

I knew that Kris really was capable of compromise. I'd seen that last year during the gala-planning work we had done together.

Kris said, "Well, I was thinking that maybe we could go trick-or-treating early in the evening, and then, when it starts to get really cold, we could come back to my house and have a party. That way we could do both."

Becca was studying Kris. I was thinking, *This isn't such a bad idea. In fact, it's a good idea.*

But was Becca capable of compromise?

Kris said, "You two could even help me make the invitations. It would be fun."

Becca still hadn't answered, and I could almost

see the machinery working inside her head. Becca's a lot like me; we don't like to give up on an idea. I just knew Becca was going to say, "No way," that we had to trick-or-treat the whole night, so I finally opened my mouth. "It's a pretty fun idea, Becca. I think." *Gulp.*

She glanced at me, and then I saw her face change. Becca is smart enough not to fight every single little battle. There was a long period of silence, but then I saw her face change even more.

Finally she said, "Yeah, you're right. A party after trick-or-treating might be fun. As long as we get to trick-or-treat long enough to get our bags full of candy."

Kris beamed. "We'll get plenty. And then we'll get even more at my party. My mom will let us make caramel apples or popcorn balls, whatever we want."

Becca said, "Okay," and I couldn't believe that finally something was settled. I would get to spend Halloween with *both* of my friends and not have to choose one over the other. *Whew!*

That night I watched the news report that came from Denver, and I heard that some of the ski resorts up in the mountains were beginning to make snow.

They can *make* snow, imagine that. At night when it drops below freezing, they blow artificial snow out of huge snow guns, and it turns out just like the real stuff.

Sometimes the world is so amazing.

I started thinking for the first time about ski season. It would be great to go up into the mountains and then fly downhill once again, like some skimming bird. It would be great to challenge the moguls again with Becca. We had done that for the first time last ski season, and while we weren't exactly great, we did get down them without killing ourselves.

Then I remembered. After those days of tackling the moguls with Becca, I had come home to Sprocket and told him all about it. As I remembered, that big aching ball started to grow again inside my chest. I had to get up and walk away from the living room and go flop down on my bed.

I didn't get to feel sorry for myself very long. Mom, who was so pregnant that she practically waddled around the house, asked for my help with dinner. I had to chop the chili peppers for chili and add them and other seasonings while she made a salad. Adam came in and helped me set the table. He got out all the salad dressings and put out the napkins.

"Just in time for the really hard work," I said to him with a snort.

But he didn't smile or laugh. Usually Adam and I joke back and forth while we do our never-ending chores. When Sprocket was here with us, he had always kept us company, but since Sprocket had left, Adam and I had not joked around much. The chores were just chores again. It had been Sprocket who'd made everything fun.

I wondered how Sprocket's advanced training was going. Was he doing well? Was he messing up? Did he miss me? Did he understand why we had had to send him away?

I couldn't help it. I felt something like hope spring into my chest whenever I imagined Sprocket messing up. After all, he had been very jumpy and unruly when he first came to live with us. Maybe he was like that again. Maybe the new surroundings had caused him to lose ground. Maybe he would forget all of his training. Maybe he wouldn't make it as a service dog after all. Maybe we would get him back as a pet.

I made another snide remark to Adam about setting the table being such an easy job, but he acted as if I hadn't said a word.

When we all sat down to eat, Dad asked Mom how she was feeling. She said, "Fine," but she looked exhausted. The salad she had made had big chunks of lettuce in it. Usually she chops it up fine, the way Adam and I like it.

Dad started talking about the pigs. And then the weather. No one was joining in, and I felt sorry for him. Something was just *not right*, and I couldn't wait for dinner to end. Even homework would be better than this. Tonight everyone except Dad was sad, or tired, or both.

Dad continued being his usual cheery, calm self. "What's going on with everyone tonight?" he asked and looked around.

Adam finished his salad and dug into his chili.

Mom was starting on her chili, too, but suddenly she covered her mouth.

Dad was still waiting for someone to talk to him when Adam swallowed his first spoonful of chili. He coughed, looked over at me, and squinted. "What did you put in here, oh ye queen of the chili peppers?"

I squinted right back. "What did I put in there? The peppers and the seasonings, of course. Exactly what Mom told me to put in there."

Mom coughed. "It's okay."

Adam said, "Did you measure?"

"Of course I measured. I'm not an idiot."

Mom intervened. "Chilies vary in degrees of hotness. I guess Dad picked out some heavy-duty ones at the grocery store by mistake."

Adam pushed his bowl aside. He shoved back his chair. "I think I'll get a bowl of cereal."

I tried the chili myself then.

Whoa! I had to gulp down some water. Another big gulp of water, and the fire still hadn't stopped burning on my tongue and even inside my teeth. I grabbed a piece of bread and scarfed that down.

Mom was staring into her bowl. She said softly, "I'll get heartburn if I eat this."

We all sat in silence for a moment or two.

Dad finally got up. "Guess it's a cereal night for everyone."

He came back with all the cereal boxes he could find, some fresh bowls, and the milk carton.

A few minutes later, I looked down into my bowl of Rice Krispies and then realized that I couldn't eat this, either. I was remembering how Sprocket, before he was trained not to do so, would come sniffing around the dinner table at night, looking for crumbs on the floor. Sometimes I slipped him a snack or two, but that was only in the beginning.

Dad was saying, "Maybe we should take this opportunity to choose some names for the twins."

No one responded.

Dad gave Adam and me a *look*, that look that said he was disappointed in us. "Since no one is talking about anything else," he said pointedly.

"Not in the mood," snapped Adam.

Dad looked over at me, and I could see it in his eyes. I was the reliable one, and he was trying to get me to perk up. "Snicker, do you have any ideas?"

Dad always calls me Snicker when he wants to cheer me up. But I had to say, "No," because it was the truth.

Dad went on, "Do you think the names should rhyme? Or start with the same letter?"

"NO," I said. "Definitely not either one of those. The twins will sound like toys or something."

"Okay, so what are two boys' names that you like?" Dad asked. "We'll start there."

Boys' names? I wondered if Dad knew that the twins were boys.

But instead of drilling him or Mom, which I knew would be of no use, I shrugged. "I like Matthew."

Adam piped up, "Matthew is the name of the

biggest twerp in my class. No way."

I said, "I also like Justin."

Silence.

Dad said, "I'm not crazy about Justin."

Silence, again.

Adam slammed down his spoon. "What about Sprocket? I mean, that's a great name for a dog. So, why not for a kid, too?" He was glaring at everybody, especially Mom. All of a sudden I knew he was going to say all the things I couldn't say. I knew it was all about to pour out.

He glowered at Mom. "You shouldn't have done this to us. We should never have taken a dog only to give him away later. Don't ever take a service dog in training again. Never, ever."

He threw down his napkin and stormed away from the table.

I just sat there. Now I knew I wasn't going to eat for sure.

Mom was just sitting there. Dad, too.

Mom finally spoke in her soft, understanding voice. "I didn't know it would be so hard on the two of you," she said to me. "But believe it or not, the best thing to do *is* to train another dog."

I couldn't even look at her.

Thanks to Nicki

That night in my journal, I wrote:

I love my mother and all, and most of the time she's really smart. But this time I don't believe her.

8

Halloween and the Day After

On Halloween night, Becca dressed as a hobbit, and Kris dressed as some kind of princess from outer space. From her spot on the couch, Mom helped me put together an outfit that made me look like one of those Irish dancers—you know, the ones who move their feet so fast and tap like crazy.

It was a great costume for me this particular Halloween. I figured that I might have to make some fast moves to get Becca and Kris to be nice to each other. After finally compromising on what we would do this Halloween, they had gone back to arguing, just as before.

We started out in town, where Becca's mother dropped us off to trick-or-treat on the block where we always start. There were tons of kids in costumes; some I recognized, but more I didn't. The little kids went up to each door while their parents waited on the sidewalk.

Becca and I led Kris around the neighborhood where we had always received good treats, and Kris surprised me by saying, "This is fun," a couple of times. We got bags full of candy and other things that

I held back to let Becca lead the way on her own.

I knew Mom would say we should eat slowly, over several weeks. "Too much sugar," she says every year. But then every year she seems to enjoy helping Adam and me eat our sugary treats!

Then I held back to let Becca lead the way on her own, which seemed to make her happy. That way I could spend some time walking and talking with Kris. After finishing up at our favorite house, we met up with Kris's mom, who drove us back to Kris's house.

It was a party like no party I'd ever been to. Kris and her parents had decorated their enormous house with Halloween stuff, complete with spiderwebs everywhere and jillions of lighted pumpkins and bowls of freshly made treats. We got to play any music we wanted, and just about every girl in our class was there. We even got up off the couches and chairs and danced to the good songs. At one point, Becca and Kris danced with each other, and it was almost as though they forgot for a minute to fight over me.

Some of the other girls started calling us "the three of you" or "you three," and I thought that maybe my plan was actually working. Maybe we *were* becoming a threesome after all.

And then the most amazing thing of all happened.

I had a good time, and for a few minutes, I forgot to miss Sprocket.

The next day was a school day like any other, except that all the girls were talking about what a great party Kris had thrown. For a minute I was jealous of Kris, because of her huge house and all that money. She didn't have to do ranch chores like Becca and I did. But at the same time, I was happy for Kris. And I liked it that she wasn't stuck-up about living in such a great house.

After school, Mom was waiting for me, and I could tell by the look on her face that she had something to tell me. I just didn't know what it was yet. She asked me to sit down, which was always a bad sign.

I grabbed a box of juice from the refrigerator and perched on the edge of the couch in the living room, preparing myself.

Knowing me so well, Mom started with, "This is *good* news, Nicki, although I'm not sure *you're* going to see this as good news." She sighed. "In time I'm certain that you'll see this as a great thing."

"Just go ahead and say it, Mom."

She had to sigh one more time. "Well, I heard from Mrs. Tate that Sprocket completed his advanced training."

Killer. I had to look down at the floor and will my eyes not to explode.

Mom said, "He has been partnered with a child who lives in Denver and who uses a wheelchair. A girl."

I swallowed a few times, hard.

A few long, agonizing moments passed. Every breath I took felt like a stab at my heart.

All I could say was, "Great."

"You know, Nicki, this was the whole purpose all along. I'm just sorry that you got so attached to Sprocket."

Oh boy. "Attached?" I glared at her. I couldn't help it. "I love that dog, Mom. You know it."

"I *do* know it, and that just goes to show what a warm and loving person you are, but as I said, this *was* the purpose all along. As much as it hurts now, I know that you'll see that in the end."

"In the end?" I screeched. "This *is* the end!"

"Of course it's *not* the end. In fact, we can train another dog soon, if you like."

"No!" I yelled. "No way!"

Mom remained calm. "I'm sorry you feel that way, Nicki. But in time . . ."

I wouldn't even think about that.

Dad walked in and kicked off his work boots. "Congratulations, Nicki," he said.

I grunted in response.

He raised an eyebrow and continued, "Well, grunt or no grunt, you really did it. You did something special that I bet no other kid you know has done." He waited a minute. "I'm proud of you. I'm proud of my girl."

But praise wouldn't work on me.

Mom finally spoke again. "We're making your favorite dinner tonight to celebrate. Spaghetti and meatballs with lots of buttery garlic bread."

I made myself smile at her, because I could see how hard she was trying, and I knew I was just taking it out on her now. And that wasn't fair.

But for once in my life I could hardly eat Mom's great spaghetti and meatballs. I couldn't even eat the garlic bread.

The next morning when my alarm went off, I pushed the alarm button all the way down, rolled over, and buried my head in the pillows. When Mom came by, she stood at the doorway. "Up and at 'em, Nicki. It's already late."

I spoke from the hush of the pillows. "I don't feel so good, Mom."

She paused. "What's wrong?"

"My stomach feels funny. Like maybe I'm going to throw up."

"Oh," she said and stood there, thinking. I can always hear Mom thinking. "Maybe you should stay home today."

Good.

"Yeah," I mumbled back.

"I'll call the attendance office at school," Mom said and then reached down and tucked me in, no small feat for her with her huge belly full of twins. "You go back to sleep now, and just call me if you need me. Okay?"

"Okay."

Then it was back to dream time. I slept off and on for the whole day. I got up only to eat the chicken soup Mom made me for lunch. I gulped down the soup, because by then I hadn't eaten much in almost twenty-four hours. The soup tasted good—the noodles were all slippery and tender.

I cleaned out the bowl, and then I realized that of course it wasn't my *stomach* that was sick. It was my heart. Now I knew it all for sure, everything that I had feared.

Sprocket would never be mine again.

Mrs. Tate had invited Mom and me to attend
a graduation ceremony for the dogs that had passed
advanced training. There we could officially hand over
Sprocket to the girl who was getting him, but I had
said, "No." I couldn't imagine doing such a thing and
not crying. And I was sick of crying. I didn't want to
do it ever again.

After school I received two calls, one from Becca
and one from Kris, each of them asking why I had
missed school and how I was feeling, that sort of thing.
I could tell that Mom must have told them about
Sprocket passing his advanced training, because there
was something kind of sad and knowing in the way
they talked to me. It was nice to find out that they
could actually think about *me* for a minute and not
be competing for me, but I didn't know what to say.
I really just needed to be left alone.

And so I looked out my window to the mountains
that had so far received only a few dustings of snow.
Although the ski resorts were busy making artificial
snow, they probably wouldn't open for the season until

a big storm dumped a lot of snow.

If only it would snow big, I mean *really* snow big, then I could think about skiing again instead of thinking about Sprocket. Gliding down the mountain was probably the only thing that was going to make me feel better.

I made myself get up and go to school on Monday, even though I really didn't want to. It had been so much easier to just sleep it all away.

But once I got to school, I realized what a big mistake I'd made. Everyone KNEW. And I had called even more attention to it by staying home the Friday before.

I could see it in their faces and hear it in their voices. Everyone knew that Sprocket wasn't coming back, and everyone felt sorry for me. It would've been easier if they had all acted as though it were any day, just any old normal day. But all those looks and sympathetic smiles made me feel worse.

People said some nice things, such as "Good job, Nicki," that made me want to hide in a corner. Other kids started telling me stories about lost pets or animals that had died, and then I *really* wanted to hide in a corner. I guess they were trying to help, but all I could do was nod.

Mr. Thomas was the only one who was acting normal. He told us that we had a really tough schedule of work to get through, and then he proceeded to give us one assignment after another. There was hardly any time for anything else. He just kept pounding away so that we barely got a recess break, and then he asked us to discuss our social studies subject during lunchtime.

Then it occurred to me. He was doing it on purpose. For me.

He was keeping everyone busy so that they wouldn't talk about my dog that wasn't going to be my dog ever again. No congratulations or celebrations, just lots of work so that no one would have much opportunity for chatter. Who would've thought it? Mr. Thomas—he was the only person who really got it.

I felt like going up and hugging him.

In my journal that night I wrote:

Maybe he's not so bad as a teacher after all.

9

Birth Day

Two nights later, Dad woke me up in the middle of the night.

"Nicki," he said as he nudged me gently awake. "Your mother has gone into labor. I'm taking her to the hospital. You and Adam will be alone for a while."

In a flash I was wide-awake. I sat up straight in bed. "I want to go."

Dad paused for only a moment. I could see that he was anxious to leave. He said, "We can't leave Adam alone."

I pushed back my covers and sprang out of bed. "I'll wake him up."

And so it ended up that Adam and I threw on some clothes and shoes, and then the whole family rode to the hospital.

I didn't know what to expect out of a woman in labor about to have twins, but Mom was amazingly calm. She got real quiet at times as we rode into town, and at other times she breathed kind of hard and held on to her huge belly, but I could tell she was okay.

Dad kept looking over at her and checking as he drove the car at the speed limit all the way to the hospital. Then he parked outside the emergency entrance and went in. A nurse came out with a wheelchair for Mom. I guess they didn't want her to walk.

Adam and I got to ride the elevator up to the Obstetrics floor, but then we had to wait in a special lobby for families of women in labor. Dad got to go all the way inside, beyond those pale green swinging doors.

Then it was silent, like the middle of the night again, only with no dreams. Adam sat down and pulled out one of his handheld video games. At least he had thought to bring something to do.

I looked at the clock. 3:16 A.M.

I looked around and found a stack of magazines on the table in the room. I tried looking through a few of them, but they were boring, and I couldn't get my mind off what Mom might be going through. Would she and the twins be okay?

"Would you stop it?" Adam said.

I spun around and said, "Stop what?"

"Pacing the floor."

I looked down at my feet. I hadn't known I had been pacing the floor. But then I realized I had been walking around the room in circles, around and around that table with all the boring magazines on it.

I said to Adam, "How can you be so calm?"

He shrugged and kept looking at his game screen. "Nothing I can do about it."

"You could at least worry along with me."

He snorted. "No way, José. You go on worrying without me."

And so I did.

Dad came out once about 5:30 A.M. and told us that everything was going well and that it might be over soon. Then he disappeared again very quickly.

Adam was still playing his game, and now I could hear little beeping sounds coming out of it. Boy, I wished his battery would go dead.

Finally, at 6:45, Dad came out beaming. "Two girls," he said. "Two sisters!"

Something lurched inside my chest. Girls? Just as I had secretly hoped? It was too good to be true!

I ran up and hugged Dad. "Is everything okay?"

"Perfect," he answered. "They're even bigger than we had hoped, weighing in at about four and

one-half pounds apiece, and your mother is doing
swell. No problems with her, either."

I bounced up and down on my toes. "When can
we see them?"

Dad said, "In a while. I'll come back for you."

"What do they look like?"

"You'll see," Dad said before he scurried away.

Geez, I was stuck with Adam again.

Finally he looked up from his game. "Two more
sisters," he said. "Great."

I snorted at him.

We got to see Mom before we saw the babies.
Dad came out and led Adam and me into her hospital
room, where she was sitting up in bed wearing a
hospital gown. The sun was just starting to light up the
mountains outside the window as Adam and I gently
hugged Mom. She looked really tired but happy.

Mom had work for us to do. She said, "We have
to get serious about names now. If everything goes
well, all three of us might be able to go home tomorrow
or the next day, and we have to fill out the birth certifi-
cates before we're discharged from the hospital. Right
now the twins are with the nurses, but you'll see them
soon enough."

We all agreed it was finally time to make some

decisions. None of us wanted Mom to worry about it.

So Adam and I perched on the edge of the bed on either side of Mom, and Dad pulled up a chair.

He said, "I've always liked Elizabeth for a girl. What about Elizabeth for one and maybe something like Vanessa for the other?"

Adam shook his head. "Too long. Too girly."

"Yeah," I agreed. "Those names sound kind of prissy to me."

Adam said, "What about May and June, you know, like the months?"

I glared at him. This was no time for jokes.

"Those are real names, you know," said Dad. "From a long time ago."

Adam continued, "Or we could do places, you know, like Cheyenne and Dakota."

I glared even harder.

Dad said, "Those are real names, too."

"Yeah," I said. "But I don't want them for *our* twins."

"Okay," he said. "So you come up with some ideas."

I looked at Mom. "Mom did all the work. Let's let her choose."

Mom shook her head. "I can't. Really, I'm just

too tired to think. Besides, we'll get used to any names.
We just have to pick some." She looked upward.
"Please just pick some."

"But it's important," I said.

"Then you choose," she said and looked at me.
"You'll be the big sister, and these two girls are always
going to look up to you for that. It'll be really special
for them if they know that you chose their names. You
can take some time to figure it out, but we all need to
agree before the day's out."

"I like that idea," said Dad.

"Fine by me," Adam piped up.

I looked at Dad, and for a moment he had the
strangest look on his face. It was like this huge combination of joy and sadness at the same time. Then I
knew what he was thinking. They were all trying, still,
to help ease the pain of losing Sprocket. That's why
they were giving me something really special to do.

Adam and I got to stay at the hospital all day
long and miss a day of school. We ate breakfast and
lunch in the hospital cafeteria with Dad while they
brought Mom trays of food in her room. Between
breakfast and lunch, the pediatrician was finally
through checking the twins, and they were placed in
bassinets in the nursery window for us to see. Wow,

were they ever tiny. Each one a whole human being in just four and one-half pounds. But they had chubby little perfect faces that peeked out from the layers of blankets the nurses had wrapped them in. Both were sleeping as though they had had a tough night, too.

I guess it's a lot of work being born, especially when you don't get the whole show to yourself and have to share it with a twin.

I just stood there and stared for a long time. It felt kind of miraculous that two new people had just emerged into the world. One day we hadn't been able to see them or imagine what they looked like, and then in just a few hours, here they were—all wonderful and warm and sweet—everything I'd hoped they would be.

Now I just needed to find the right names.

After school, Becca and Kris came together to visit us at the hospital. They stood on either side of me at the nursery window and stared at the twins.

"Oh, my gosh," said Kris, "they are so cute."

Becca agreed. "Wow," she said. "Pretty tiny faces, for sure."

"What did your parents name them?" asked Kris,

turning toward me.

I was so tired from getting up in the middle of the night that I had almost forgotten. I yawned and said, "We haven't named them yet. We can't agree, and so earlier today, my mother put me in charge. I have to choose the names."

"But that's so cool," said Kris, "*really* cool, Nicki! I'm jealous. Your parents trust you a lot."

Becca said, "Yeah, what an honor."

I lifted my hands and then let them fall. "But I have no ideas at the moment."

Becca said, "Let's go to the gift shop. When my aunt had her baby here, we saw some baby name books in the gift shop."

I thought that was a fine plan.

On the way down to the gift shop, we all agreed that the twins' names shouldn't rhyme and also shouldn't start with the same letter. They were identical twins but they should have their own unique names.

"It's better to be a little different," said Becca.

Kris smiled and nodded.

And I couldn't have agreed more.

The volunteer at the counter in the gift shop let us look through a baby name book without buying it, and we found that half the book contained girls' names. Okay, so that was a start. Then the book was divided into chapters based on nationality, such as English names, German names, etc.

Boy, were there a lot of names! And I was getting sleepier by the minute.

But then one chapter caught my attention. It was entitled "Arthurian Legend Names." Lately, we had been reading King Arthur's story in school, and I loved it. So did Becca and Kris. So we ended up concentrating on that chapter.

We started down the list.

We liked Anna, the name of Arthur's sister, and we also liked Elaine, the name of Arthur's mother. Both names were pretty and I was close to choosing them, but then the greatest idea of all hit me—something *really* special, and something that could help solve another problem.

I looked at Becca. "I've got it," I said. "Rebecca for one of the twins—like you, Becca, only a little different, you know, so that everyone can tell who I'm talking about."

Becca beamed.

Then I looked at Kris. "And Kristine for the other twin. Almost like your name, Kris."

I thought for a minute that she was going to cry.

"Are you sure, Nicki?" Kris asked. "I mean, that's a real honor."

Becca agreed. "It lasts a lifetime, too . . . Maybe you shouldn't."

I said, "But you are my two best friends."

Rebecca and Kristine.

Becca and Kris smiled so big, and their eyes were all shiny. "Thank you," they said at the same time, and then laughed.

Boy, what a great feeling! Becca, Kris, and I put the name book back on the shelf, and then I hugged them both on either side of me. We were all so excited that the weirdest thing happened. All of a sudden Kris and Becca moved around and hugged each other, too, and we formed a circle. A circle of three. And there was nothing fake about it. My plan had worked. We had actually become a trio.

Back up in Mom's room, I told Mom and Dad the names I'd picked for the twins, and they loved them! Even Adam said they were "Okay," which was a big compliment for him.

Birth Day

Later the nurses brought the twins into Mom's room and put one into her arms. Mom looked down at that twin and said, "Rebecca."

Another nurse put the second twin into Dad's arms. He said, "Kristine."

I thought I might sob, but I gulped it back. That ache that had been in my chest ever since Sprocket left was still there, and now it was throbbing.

But then Mom told me to sit beside her on the bed, and when I did, she asked Dad to slide the bundle that was Kristine into my arms. She showed how to support Kristine's head, and then I just sat there and

looked down at Kristine's tiny pink, perfect face. For the first time, that ache that had lived inside of me for so long eased just the tiniest bit.

That night it occurred to me that it had been one of the longest days of my life, but also one of the happiest. I remembered holding Kristine in my arms and thought about what had happened to the pain in my chest when I was holding my baby sister.

In my journal, I wrote:

It stopped for only a second or so. But it's a beginning.

10

The Visit

By the twins' one-month birthday, they had already gained over a pound apiece and were doing great. At night I helped bathe them and rock them to sleep, but Mom and Dad were taking turns doing all of the middle-of-the-night feedings and changings. Most of the time I just snoozed right through all of that late-night activity.

In the mornings I kissed Rebecca and Kristine good-bye before I went to school. They could almost focus on a face, and when they saw me, I could tell that Mom was right. I was going to be the big BIG sister for life.

The day after the twins' one-month hurrah, I woke up and the first thing I said to Mom was, "I want to visit Sprocket."

She looked at me with that *mother* look in her eyes. "You wouldn't go to the graduation ceremony. You said 'No.'"

"Yeah," I said and cringed a bit. "I said 'No' too fast, maybe? Or maybe I just need to change my mind?"

Mom smiled.

So a few days later Mrs. Tate drove out to the ranch and took Mom and me to visit Sprocket in his new home. She had called and worked it out. We were invited to visit Sprocket and Laura, his new owner, at her home in Denver. For a moment before we left I thought that maybe I shouldn't have suggested this. I didn't know what to expect of me, Mom, Sprocket, anyone. It might make it all awful again. It might make everything worse.

But we went anyway.

Dad was watching the twins, and Adam decided to stay with Dad. He had sort of adopted the theory Kris had once advised and had bought himself a hamster he named Chip. Chip was brown and white and very tame. Adam took him out of his cage and held him in his hands and even let him run up and down his arms. Adam had fallen in love with a rodent, something farm and ranch kids don't often do. But it was working for him.

It was a cloudy day with low gray mist moving in. I had to really bundle up for the first time all fall with a hat, boots, and gloves. If only it would just go ahead and snow.

The exhaust from Mrs. Tate's car looked like a

frosty fog puffing out into the air, and Mrs. Tate had to keep her windshield wipers on, because the mist was building up and beginning to freeze on the glass. As we drove toward Denver, we had to cross a mountain pass, and we could feel the temperature drop even though we were inside a warm, heated car.

All the way there, Mom and Mrs. Tate talked about service-dog training and what was happening with the organization and all that, but I just kept quiet. I stared out the window at all the fields that were now gold and brown and barren. As we climbed the pass between our valley and Denver, I watched as the scenery changed to evergreen trees and frozen streams and rocky hillsides. Then we left the trees again as we descended into Denver.

Mrs. Tate drove us to a house in a neighborhood of older homes, split-rail fences, and large landscaped yards. We pulled up in front of a house that had red brick, gray paint, and black shutters. In front there was a ramp that went over the steps, and that's when I remembered. This girl, Laura, was in a wheelchair.

A woman answered the door and ushered us into a family room, where Laura was sitting, waiting for us.

But then I saw my dog and nothing else.

My Sprocket was sitting at Laura's side, just as well-behaved as can be. He didn't run up and jump on us or anything, but I could see in his eyes that he still knew me. There were those stars in his eyes and something there like a great big *HELLO!*

Mrs. Tate introduced me to Laura, who had red hair and a million freckles and about the brightest blue eyes I'd ever seen. She was smiling as she told us to sit down. Then she showed us some of the things that Sprocket did for her. I was able to see that Sprocket now knew how to open doors and retrieve things out of the refrigerator. He must have learned those things in advanced training. He could even hand Laura the phone when it was ringing.

After he did something for her, Laura reached down and gave him lots of loving, and I could see that she really did love Sprocket. Her face broke into another smile, and Sprocket smiled back with that great big doggie grin of his. And then the most amazing thing happened. When Laura looked at Sprocket, she got stars in her eyes—stars that matched Sprocket's exactly.

They loved each other.

Sprocket was such a great dog that he had transferred his love to someone else, someone who really *did* need him more than I did.

The Visit

That's when I realized that Laura was talking to me. She was saying, "Sprocket's the best friend I've ever had. He's so loyal and obedient, and so smart. He's such a cute dog, too. All my friends love him."

"May I come over and pet him?" I asked her.

"Sure," she said.

And so I got to love on Sprocket for the first time in a long, long time. His coat felt just the same. The shine in his eyes was just the same, and the doggie grin he broke into for me was just the same, too.

Only he didn't belong to me anymore.

When I opened my eyes, Laura said in a whisper, "Thank you."

I didn't have to force myself. I said, "You're welcome."

When I said good-bye to Sprocket for the last time, *really* the last time, it was the saddest moment of my life, but then when I let him go and he went back to Laura and sat at her side just as he was supposed to, it was the best moment of my life, too.

When I got into the car with Mom and Mrs. Tate, none of us talked. We were probably all just exhausted and lost in our own thoughts. I was thinking about how it was funny—things can be really sad and really wonderful at the same time.

Thanks to Nicki

I stared out the window again back at Laura's house, and at that moment, I realized that the mist that had been falling all day was changing to fresh, heavy, powdery snow.

True
Stories

Meet some of the kids who have
service dogs as partners—and two
puppy-raising sisters in Colorado.

Nikita, Morell, and Nikita's cousin, Ben, enjoy an outing together.

Nikita W. was nine years old when Morell came into her life. Morell is an assistance dog who is Nikita's almost constant companion and partner. Nikita, who lives in California, uses a wheelchair because she has a disease that can make it hard to control the muscles in her body. Morell helps Nikita by picking things up, opening doors, and even turning lights on and off. Like Sprocket, Morell was raised by volunteers and then had months of advanced training to learn everything she needs to know as a working dog.

Morell provides loving companionship, but her most important job is to build Nikita's confidence and independence. If Nikita drops something, she doesn't have to ask

This dog is learning to open an automatic door. Soon the chair will be removed and he'll hop up and push the button with his nose.

for help because Morell will retrieve it for her. Morell has even helped Nikita improve her speech because Nikita has to give specific directions and commands to Morell. Nikita also ends up talking to a lot more people now—when she's out and about with Morell, people ask her all sorts of questions about Morell and assistance dogs!

Nikita attended a two-week training session with her mother to learn about handling and taking care of service dogs. During the first week, Nikita and her mom worked with twelve different dogs—but they both fell in love with Morell, who is a golden retriever. They were ecstatic when the assistance-dog trainers agreed that Nikita and Morell were good partners. "We knew that Morell was the dog for us," says Nikita's mom.

Morell is an important part of Nikita's family, both when Morell's working and when she's off-duty. Morell enjoys downtime with the family, but when she is dressed for work in her service-dog vest, she's all business, ready to help Nikita in any way she can!

Shea M., who lives across the country in Virginia, also was paired with an assistance dog when she was nine years old. Her dog, Mercer, a

Shea and Mercer

black Labrador mix, often goes to school with her. They ride the bus together, and Mercer carries Shea's lunch, picks up her pencils, opens doors, and watches out for her. "All day long, Mercer might look like he's sleeping next to my desk, but he's always got his

Shea and Mercer on their way to school

eye on me," says Shea. Just as Morell does for Nikita, Mercer makes it possible for Shea to get around by herself. With Mercer's help, using a wheelchair doesn't stop Shea from being a regular kid. "Instead of being known as the girl with the wheelchair, I'm the girl with the dog. We're a great team."

Knowing that people like Nikita and Shea will live more independent lives with the help of assistance dogs is part of what makes volunteer puppy raisers put so much heart and energy into the dogs they help train. Like Nicki, sisters Celia and Abby B., from Colorado, know what it's like to say good-bye to a dog they've come to know and love. Celia and Abby helped their mother raise Elan *(EE-lahn)*, their first assistance dog-in-training. For more than a year Elan was part of their everyday lives, and they raised and trained him with love and gentle

Puppy raisers Celia and Abby with Elan

guidance. Celia and Abby helped Elan learn about thirty commands—from "Sit" and "Stay" to "Dress," "Hurry," and "Roll"— and exposed him to many of the different experiences a service dog must be able to handle.

Elan's blue cape with yellow trim shows that he is in advanced training.

When it was time to turn Elan over to the service-dog organization for advanced training, Celia went to California with her mother. There, she participated in a graduation ceremony before saying good-bye to Elan. "Turn-in was hard, but I was really proud that we got Elan there," says Celia. Getting another puppy, Terese, one week later helped ease the loss of Elan. "Terese was a yapping ball of joy!" says Celia. "She's also really smart, and picks up commands really easily." Terese seems to be a dog who likes to work and

Abby and Celia welcome eight-week-old Terese

who is eager for new experiences—both excellent qualities in an assistance dog.

But even with Terese there, says Abby, "The house feels a bit empty without Elan." When they got the news that Elan had been released from advanced training, which happens to about 70%

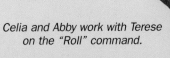

Celia and Abby work with Terese on the "Roll" command.

of the service dogs in training, the family could have adopted him as a pet but decided not to. "We didn't want to become collectors of dogs—and besides, we have a lot to do to raise and train Terese," says Celia. They were very happy to learn that Elan was immediately adopted as a pet by a loving family.

Roger responds to the "Lap" command by putting his elbows up and in his trainer Becky's lap.

One way Celia and Abby have found to keep from getting too attached to Terese—and

therefore too sad when she must leave for advanced training—is to focus on the community service they're providing as puppy raisers. For Celia, it's "knowing that someone else's life will be made better by having an assistance dog that makes all the difference."

People with many different types of disabilities can benefit from the help and companionship of a service dog.

Raising Canines

Visit these Web sites to find out what it takes to become a
puppy raiser or a service-dog trainer or about other ways to
help those who are raising assistance dogs:

You can learn more about Canine Companions for Independence,
the organization that Celia and Abby's family is working with, by
visiting their Web site at **www.cci.org**.

Find out about one of the programs that works specifically with
shelter dogs by visiting **www.freedomservicedogs.org**.

There are programs and organizations that provide assistance dogs in
just about every state. Visit **www.wags.net** to see what the Wisconsin
Academy for Graduate Service Dogs (WAGS) is up to.

CCI Basic Commands List

The puppies that Celia and Abby have been raising are from Canine Companions for Independence, a program that provides assistance dogs to people with special needs. These are the basic commands and skills that CCI puppy raisers are asked to teach their pups before turning them in for advanced training with skilled handlers. How many of these skills does *your* dog know?

The dog's name is used to get the dog's attention.

Back tells the dog to walk backwards or back up.

Bed tells the dog to go to the targeted bed and lie down.

Car tells the dog to get into the car.

Don't/No tells the dog to stop what it is doing.

Down tells the dog to lie down.

Dress tells the dog to remain still while you place a collar, halter, or cape on it.

Drop tells the dog to drop whatever is in its mouth and not pick it up again.

Heel tells the dog to move to your LEFT side and sit beside you facing forward.

Here tells the dog to come directly to you.

Hurry tells the dog it is an appropriate time and place to toilet.

Jump tells the dog to jump on top of something.

Kennel tells the dog to enter its crate or kennel.

Lap tells the dog to place its front legs across your lap, resting on its elbows.

Let's go tells the dog to walk beside you (on your left or right side) on a loose leash.

Off tells the dog to jump down or get off something.

Okay tells the dog it may eat from the food bowl.

Quiet tells the dog to stop barking.

Release tells the dog that it is free to do as it wishes within the realm of appropriate behavior.

Roll tells the dog to roll over on its back, exposing its underside.

Shake tells the dog to place its paw in the palm of your or someone else's hand.

Side tells the dog to move to your RIGHT side and sit beside you facing forward.

Sit tells the dog to put its rear on the ground.

Speak tells the dog to bark.

Stand tells the dog to stand on all four feet without walking around.

Stay tells the dog to remain in its exact position.

Turn tells the dog to turn and face the opposite direction.

Under tells the dog to go all the way under an object, such as a desk, and then lie down.

Up tells the dog to place its front paws on an object such as a table, wall, counter, etc.

Visit tells the dog to rest its chin on your lap.

Wait tells the dog not to cross a threshold or barrier.

Meet the Author

Ann Howard Creel lives outside Denver, Colorado. In addition to being an author, she is a school nurse. Her first books with American Girl were *A Ceiling of Stars* and *Nowhere Now Here*, a book about alpaca farmers. She also wrote *Nicki*, the first book in this two-book series. She has three sons and a dog and a cat and loves the mountains as much as Nicki does.